The Wrong Robber Mystery

Elaine Pageler

High Noon Books
Novato, California

Cover Design and Interior Illustrations: Tina Cash

Copyright ©1994, by High Noon Books, 20 Commercial Blvd., Novato, CA 94949-6191. All rights reserved. Printed in the United States of America. No part of this publication may be reproduced, stored in a retrieval system, or transmitted, in any form or by any means, electronic, mechanical photocopying, recording or otherwise, without the prior written permission of the publisher.

International Standard Book Number: 0-87879-985-0

9 8 7 6 5
4 3 2 1 0 9 8 7

You'll enjoy all the High Noon Books. Write for a free full list of titles.

Contents

1 The Riddle Street Team 1

2 The Briefcase 7

3 The Bank Camera 13

4 Anna's Story 20

5 More Problems 27

6 The Magic Show 32

7 The Riddle is Solved 39

CHAPTER 1

The Riddle Street Team

Brad Jones worked for the City News. He took pictures for them.

His boss had given him a new job. He was to do stories about Riddle Street. This was Brad's big break. He should be happy. But he wasn't.

It was because of Meg Green. He had to work with that pest. They were the Riddle Street team. That's what the boss said. Brad took the pictures. Meg did the writing.

"I want the first story soon," the boss said.

Brad and Meg walked down Riddle Street. They needed a story.

"Here's my idea," Meg started to say.

Brad didn't want to hear it. Meg was bossy. But she wouldn't tell him what to do.

Up ahead, he saw Anna Lopez. She went into the bank. Anna was a cute girl. She wasn't a pest like Meg. He would wait until she came out. Maybe he would ask her for a date.

"I'll take some pictures. There might be a story here," he said. Brad pulled up his camera and looked around.

A bench sat near the street. It was for bus riders. Behind it was a tree and a trash can.

They were close to him.

"Where's the story? There's nothing here," Meg told him.

Brad turned his back. "Snap, snap, snap," went his camera.

An old man stopped with a box of pens. He leaned against the bank. "Pens for sale," he called.

"Here's our story," Brad said. He walked over to the old man.

"Do you want a pen?" the old man asked.

"No, I just want to talk," Brad told him.

"Move on. I'm busy," the old man said.

Meg grinned. "That's a story?" she asked.

Then the bank door opened. Anna came out. She had a bag in her hand.

Brad ran over. "Hi, Anna, where are you going?" he asked.

Anna was in a hurry. "I must get back to work. I forgot my lunch this morning. Mom took it to work. I came over to the bank to get it," she said.

Brad watched her race away.

Meg laughed. "Cheer up. There may be a story here after all," she said.

"Where?" Brad asked.

"Look at that trash can. Why does it say CRASH? We'll build a story about it. It's a mystery of Riddle Street," Meg said.

Brad looked through his camera. It made things seem bigger.

"*Oh dear, I took a picture!*"

5

"That's no riddle. The can is bent. So the T looks like a C. Here take a look," Brad said. He handed her the camera.

Meg looked through it. "I guess you're right," she said.

"Snap," went the camera.

"Oh, dear! I took a picture," Meg said. But she didn't look sorry.

Brad grabbed his camera. He hung it around his neck.

Just then the door burst open. A man ran out. He had a briefcase. Then an alarm went off. It came from inside the bank.

A cold chill raced up Brad's back. Did this man rob the bank?

CHAPTER 2

The Briefcase

The banker raced out the door. "Help! we've been robbed!" he called.

The other man put his head down and kept going. He ran past Brad and Meg. The briefcase was tight in his arms.

Brad pulled up his camera. "Snap, snap, snap," it went.

"Bang!" came a loud sound.

Was it a gun? Brad spun around to look. So did Meg and the banker.

It was just the trash man. He was dropping trash in the truck.

Brad turned back. By now the man was at the bench. Next he would get to the street.

A police car raced up. Two men jumped out. They aimed guns at the man.

The man stopped. "What's wrong?" he asked.

One of the policemen turned to the banker. "I'm Sergeant Ward. What's going on?" he asked.

"He robbed my bank," the banker said.

"No, I didn't," said the man.

Sergeant Ward searched him. "What's your name? Why were you going so fast?" he asked.

"My name is Gil Barnes. I was rushing

back to work," the man said.

Meg poked Brad. "Did you hear that? He's acting as if he didn't do it," she said.

"Shhh! I want to hear," Brad told her.

"Let's see what's in your briefcase," Sergeant Ward said.

He opened it. There was money inside.

"There it is! That's our money!" the banker said.

Gil pulled a slip from his pocket. "No, that's my money. I cashed my pay check. It was for $400. I put $200 in the bank and took $200 in cash," he said.

Sergeant Ward looked at the money and the slip. "He's right. There is only $200 in the briefcase. The slip has today's date."

"Where's our money?" asked the banker.

Sergeant Ward turned to Brad. "Hi, Brad. I haven't seen you and Meg in a long time. Did you see Gil come out of the bank?"

"Yes, and so did Meg," Brad told him.

"Good, I want to talk to you," Sergeant Ward said. Then he turned to the old man.

"You don't need to talk to me. I don't know anything," the old man called.

"Yes, I do," said Sergeant Ward.

"I have a room inside. Would you like to use it?" the banker asked.

"Thanks," said the sergeant.

Everyone went inside. The banker took

them to a big room. It had tables and chairs.
Then he brought in Anna's mother, Mrs. Lopez.

She looked at Gil. "That's the man! He took
the money from me," Mrs. Lopez said.

"Just tell us what happened," Sergeant
Ward told her.

"That man came in. There was a gun in his
briefcase. He had a check. It was for $400. He
wanted $200 in cash and $10,000 more. I gave
it to him. He put it in the briefcase and left. I
pushed the alarm," Mrs. Lopez said.

Sergeant Ward took the briefcase. He
pulled out the $200. Then he looked inside. His
hands went all over it.

"There's no money here," he told them.

The banker shook his head. "This doesn't make sense," he said.

Sergeant Ward looked at Brad. "Brad, did you see anything?" he asked.

"Meg and I were outside the bank. This man came out with the briefcase," Brad said.

"Yes, he went right past us," Meg added.

Sergeant Ward turned to the old man. "What's your name?" he asked.

"My name is Ed. I saw Gil come out with the briefcase. That's all," the old man said.

"This is a real mystery," Meg told Brad.

Brad nodded.

"Good, that's our story. Now we have to solve it," Meg said.

CHAPTER 3

The Bank Camera

Brad watched Gil Barnes. This guy was his age. Did he rob the bank? Where was the money?

Mrs. Lopez kept saying the same thing. "He put the money in his briefcase," she told them.

"Do you know what I think? Mrs. Lopez leaned on the alarm. It was a mistake. Now Mrs. Lopez is afraid to tell you. So she made up this story," Gil said.

"No, $10,000 is gone. I checked it myself," the banker said.

"Then Mrs. Lopez took it," Gil said.

Brad jumped to his feet. "Mrs. Lopez is a good woman. She wouldn't do that," he said.

"She must have because I didn't. Do you want to search me again?" Gil asked.

Sergeant Ward shook his head. He turned to look at Mrs. Lopez. So did the banker.

Brad didn't like the looks on their faces. Did they think she took the money?

"Does your bank have cameras?" Sergeant Ward asked the banker.

"Yes, we do. They take pictures of all that goes on," the banker told him.

The banker left and came back with the film. "Here's the part where Gil comes in," he said.

Everyone watched. They saw Gil walk up. He handed Mrs. Lopez a check. She gave him a slip and some money. No one could see how much. Gil put the money in the briefcase. Then he put the slip in his pocket. Next, he closed the briefcase and left.

"Where was his gun?" Sergeant Ward asked.

"It's in the briefcase," Mrs. Lopez said.

The banker ran the film again. Everyone stared at it.

"See, his hand is in the briefcase. He is holding a gun," Mrs. Lopez said.

Brad watched. Gil only used one hand. The other was in his briefcase. Yes, he could be holding a gun. But no one could see it.

"I don't use that hand much. It hurts. So I rested it in the briefcase. But I didn't have a gun," Gil said.

Meg poked Brad. "Someone's lying!" she told him.

Brad knew that. He didn't need Meg to tell him. Mrs. Lopez had to be telling the truth. But where was the money and Gil's gun?

"Why do you keep checking me? Roll the film back. Let's see what Mrs. Lopez was doing?" Gil said.

They watched the film again. This time it started farther back. A man came up. He gave Mrs. Lopez a check. She gave him money. Another man stepped up. He had lots of coins.

16

Mrs. Lopez took them and gave him bills. Then Anna walked up. She didn't give Mrs. Lopez anything. Mrs. Lopez gave her a bag.

"Hold it! What's that?" Sergeant Ward asked.

"That's the $10,000. It's hidden in a bag. So there's where it went," Gil said.

"No, it's not! That's my girl's lunch," Mrs. Lopez told them.

"That's right! Anna told me she came to get her lunch," Brad said.

Sergeant Ward looked at each of them. "Who's Anna?" he asked.

"That's my girl. She forgot her lunch. So I brought it with me. She works close by," Mrs.

Lopez told him.

Sergeant Ward looked at Brad. "Do you know anything about this?" he asked.

"I know Anna. She and her mother live on my street. I saw her come out of the bank. She told me the same thing," Brad said.

"Did Anna have a bag?" Sergeant Ward asked.

"Yes, she did," Brad said.

"Anna was in a hurry," Meg added.

Sergeant Ward raised his eyebrows. "Where was she going?" he asked.

"Anna went back to work," Brad said.

Mrs. Lopez handed Sergeant Ward a card. "Here is Anna's phone number. Give her a call.

She'll tell you that was her lunch," she told him.

"Maybe she hasn't eaten it yet," Brad said.

Sergeant Ward walked out to another room. He went to phone Anna.

Everyone sat very still. Mrs. Lopez bent her head and waited. Brad felt sorry for her. But Anna would tell Sergeant Ward the truth.

Gil had a half smile on his face. His eyes darted around.

The door opened. Sergeant Ward walked back into the room.

"What did Anna say?" Brad asked.

Sergeant Ward didn't smile back. "Anna went to lunch an hour ago. She hasn't come back yet," he said.

CHAPTER 4

Anna's Story

Sergeant Ward looked at everyone. "We're trying to find Anna. A policeman is at her work place. Other men are watching the trains, buses and planes. We'll get her. But it may take time. So all of you can go home," he said.

"What? Gil robbed the bank! Mrs. Lopez said so. How can you let him go free?" Brad asked.

"I can't prove that. There's no more we can do now. I need to hear Anna's story," Sergeant Ward told them.

"Good," the old man said. He got up. Sergeant Ward took out a notepad. "Just tell me where you live and your phone number. Then you're all free to go."

Gil grinned. "I thought you would see it that way. May I have my briefcase?" he asked.

"Sure, the $200 is yours. There's nothing else in it. Just don't leave town. I may want to talk to you again," Sergeant Ward said.

"Sure," Gil said. He took the briefcase and walked out.

Mrs. Lopez stood up, too. She headed back to the other room.

"Where are you going?" the banker called.

"I'm going back to work," Mrs. Lopez said.

Sergeant Ward took out a note pad.

The banker shook his head. There was a cold look in his eye. "Take some days off. Sergeant Ward needs to talk to Anna. Then I'll phone you," he said.

Brad didn't like what the banker said. He must think Mrs. Lopez took the money.

"Come on, Brad. Let's go," Meg said.

Brad took his camera. There was one picture left. He picked it up and hung it around his neck.

Meg led the way. "What a break! This is a great mystery. It happened on Riddle Street. The boss will like this," she said.

Brad stopped outside the door. He took the last picture. Then he walked up the street.

Meg came along. "Anna must have taken the money. Nothing else makes sense," she said.

Brad knew Sergeant Ward and the banker thought the same thing. Things looked very bad for Mrs. Lopez. Where was Anna?

A camera store was up ahead. Brad took his film inside. He gave it to the man.

Meg had waited outside. Now she poked her head in the door. "Brad, come here! Be quick!" she called.

Brad dashed out. "What's up?" he asked.

"Here comes Anna!" Meg said.

Brad looked down Riddle Street. Anna came their way. She was running. There was no bag in her hands.

"She's in a big hurry," said Meg.

Brad watched her come closer. "Where have you been, Anna?" he called.

Anna smiled. But she didn't slow down.

"Stop, I have to talk to you," Brad said.

"I'm late for work," she told him.

"The police are looking for you," he called after her.

"Police?" said Anna. She stopped and turned around.

"They think you robbed a bank," Brad said.

Anna's eyes got big. "Me?" she asked.

Brad told her what happened. "Sergeant Ward thinks the $10,000 was in your bag," he said.

"That was my lunch," Anna said.

Meg gave her a cool look. "Where have you been? Where is the bag?"

"You said you were going back to work. But you didn't," Brad said.

Anna's face turned red. "I didn't want to tell you about Jim. We were going to eat lunch in the park," she said.

"Then Jim knows about the bag. He saw the lunch," Brad said.

Anna shook her head. "I waited for him. But he never showed up. That's why I'm late," she told them.

"Where's the bag?" Brad asked.

"I put it in a trash can," Anna said.

CHAPTER 5

More Problems

Anna looked at Meg and Brad. "I'm no robber. You know that. Don't you?"

Brad nodded his head.

But Meg didn't. She fired questions at Anna. "Were you really at the park? Can you prove it? Did anyone see you?" she asked.

Brad frowned at Meg. She was acting like a policeman. How dare she treat Anna that way! But he waited for Anna to say something. Maybe someone had seen her. That would help.

"There were lots of people in the park. But I didn't know anyone," Anna told them.

"What about the trash can? Your bag would be in it," Brad said.

Anna led them to the park. It was only a block away. She pointed to a trash can. "There it is," she said.

The trash can sat near a table. It was filled with bags. They all looked alike.

"Was your name on it?" Brad asked.

"No, but one is mine," Anna said.

"Sergeant Ward won't think so," Brad said.

"That's right," someone said.

There stood Sergeant Ward. His eyes were on Anna and he didn't smile. "We've been looking for you," he said.

"Anna is just coming back from lunch," Brad said.

Sergeant Ward held up his hand. "Let Anna tell her own story. She and I are going down town. We will talk there," he told Brad.

A police car waited at the curb. Sergeant Ward led Anna to it. She looked back at the park. Was she looking for Jim?

"We have our story. Anna and her mother are the bank robbers," Meg said.

"No, they aren't. I know them," Brad said.

"She lied to you," Meg went on.

"Yes, and we know why. She was meeting Jim," Brad told her.

"Do you know Jim?" Meg asked.

Brad shook his head.

"Maybe there isn't a Jim. Anna just made him up," Meg said.

Brad didn't want to hear that. He turned and walked back to Riddle Street. Mrs. Lopez would be home by now. He would go talk to her.

"Wait for me," Meg called.

"Get lost," Brad called back to her.

"No way! We're the Riddle Street team. This is our story," she said.

Brad walked faster. Meg did, too.

Anna's house was just ahead. A police car was parked at the curb. It must be Sergeant Ward. Had he brought Anna home?

The front door opened. Two policemen came out with Mrs. Lopez. They led her to the car.

"Brad ran up to them. "What's going on?" he asked.

"We're taking Mrs. Lopez in. We just found the bag and one of the bills. They were in her house," the policeman told them.

Mrs. Lopez had tears in her eyes. "My back door was not locked. Someone must have put them inside," she said.

"That's right. It was Anna," the policeman said.

He closed the door and started the car.

Mrs. Lopez rolled down the window. "Help us, Brad," she called.

CHAPTER 6

The Magic Show

The next morning Brad sat at his desk. Gil was on his mind. That man had robbed the bank. But how did he do it?

Meg walked over. "I was at a party last night. I met this guy," she told him.

"Tell someone else. I'm busy," Brad said.

Meg went on talking. "His name is Jim. He likes a girl named Anna. They were going to meet in the park for lunch. But his car broke down," she told him.

32

Brad jumped up. "He's Anna's friend! That proves her story," he said.

Meg nodded. "It does to me. Jim phoned her house. But no one answered," she went on.

"Anna's in jail," Brad said.

"That's what I told him. He went to see Sergeant Ward this morning. But Sergeant Ward still thinks Anna did it," Meg said.

"Gil's the robber. But how can I prove it?" Brad asked.

"Well, I did some checking. Gil works at Sam's Shoe Store," Meg told him.

"Good girl!" Let's go," Brad said.

Sam's Shoe Store was two blocks away. It was a big store. Lots of people were inside.

A man stood near the door. He had boxes of shoes in his hand.

Brad walked over to him. "Does Gil Barnes work here?" he asked.

"Yes, but this is his day off. You'll find him at the park. He's doing a magic show there," the man said.

"He does magic?" Brad asked.

"Yes, and he's good," the man said.

Brad and Meg went to the park. The magic show wasn't hard to find. There were lots of signs. They pointed to the stage.

Gil wore a black suit. He stood by a table and did tricks. A woman was near by. She was his helper.

The woman gave him a card. Gil put a scarf over it. Then he took it off. The card was gone.

"How did he do that?" Meg asked.

"It's up his arm," Brad told her.

Next the woman brought out a vase. "Look what I bought," she said.

Gill took the vase. He put it in a box. "It costs too much. We'll send it back," he said.

The woman walked to the other side of the stage. She stood there crying. "I want that vase," she screamed.

"Oh, all right," Gil said. He opened the box. The vase was gone.

"Here it is," the woman called. She stood across the stage. The vase was in her hands.

The woman gave him a card.

Everyone clapped.

So did Meg. "How did they do that?" she asked.

"I don't know," Brad said.

"That's easy," said a man behind them.

Brad turned to him. "Will you tell us how?" he asked.

"Sure, Gil had two boxes. One was under the table. The woman walked across the stage. She screamed and everyone looked at her. No one watched Gil. That's when he changed the boxes," the man told them.

"Oh, I get it. Then we watched Gil open an empty box. No one watched the woman. She pulled out another vase," Brad said.

"That's right," said the man.

"It's a good trick. He had me fooled. I never thought of two boxes," Meg said.

Brad jumped up. "That's it, Meg! You've got it!" he said.

"What do you mean?" Meg asked.

"We never thought of two briefcases. That's how Gil did it! He had $200 in one. The other had the money from the bank. He just changed one for the other," Brad told her.

"How could he do that?" Meg asked.

Brad shook his head. "I don't know," he said.

CHAPTER 7

The Riddle Is Solved

Brad and Meg walked back down Riddle Street. They talked about Gil.

"I know I'm right. Gil did the same trick at the bank. He had two briefcases," Brad said.

"He needed a helper. Was it Ed?" Meg asked.

"I don't think so," Brad said.

The camera store was just ahead. Brad went in and got his pictures. He showed them to Meg.

First, there were pictures of Riddle Street.

Then there was a picture of Ed.

"Here's the picture I took. The trash can says CRASH," Meg said.

The next set of pictures were of Gil. First, he was at the door. Next he was close by. Then, he was by the tree and the trash can.

Meg picked up another picture. It showed a trash truck. "What's this?" she asked.

"That's when we heard the bang. I turned and took a picture," Brad told her.

The next picture showed Gil again. He was near the street. Then came pictures of Sergeant Ward and the banker. They were with Gil. The last picture showed Riddle Street again.

"That's when we came out of the bank,"

Brad said.

"Look at the trash can! This time it says TRASH!" Meg said.

"That's a new can," Brad told her.

Brad and Meg looked at one another. "The helper was the trash man!" they shouted.

"That's right. Gil had two briefcases. One had $200. Gil hid it in the trash can. Then he took the other and robbed the bank," Brad said.

"His helper waited in the trash truck," Meg added.

Brad nodded. "Yes, Gil came out. He ran over to the can. The trash man made a loud bang. We looked around and Gil changed the briefcase. Then we went in the bank. The trash man changed the cans," Brad said.

Meg picked up a picture. "Look, there's a phone number. It's on the door of the truck."

Brad phoned the trash people. "Who picks up trash on Riddle Street?" he asked.

"No one did this week. Our truck is being worked on. It's at Jack's shop. That's on the corner of Riddle and Pine," the voice said.

Next, Brad called Sergeant Ward.

Then, he and Meg dashed to Jack's Shop. There was a sign on the door. It said, "Closed."

"No one's here," Meg said.

"There's an open window. Maybe someone is inside. Let's go see," Brad said.

They walked to the window and peeked in.

There sat the trash truck, the can and two briefcases. Gil and a woman were inside. They had money in their hands.

"She's from the Magic show," Meg said.

Brad nodded. "Shhh, let's hear what they say," he told her.

"You were a great trash man," Gil said.

The woman laughed. "The cans were heavy. But I changed them," she said.

"We had luck. Your brother Jack was sick. So we could use this shop. I fixed the truck. We did our trick at the bank. Now it's time to get out of here," Gil said.

Brad looked around. "I wish Sergeant Ward would come," he said.

Just then the door crashed in. "Hands up," Sergeant Ward called.

Brad and Meg waited outside. Soon Sergeant Ward brought Gil and the woman out.

"Now we have the real robbers. Anna and her mother will go free. Thanks to you," Sergeant Ward told them.

He led Gil and the woman away.

Meg grinned at Brad. "How about that? We have a great story," she said.

Brad watched the sun shine on Meg's hair. She was still a pest. But Meg was cute at times. And she was good at solving mysteries. Maybe this new job would be OK.

"Good for the Riddle Team," Brad told her.